The Puppy Collection

Bailey's Visit

Susan Hughes

Illustrated by
Leanne Franson

Scholastic Canada Ltd.

Toronto New York London Au
Mexico City New Delhi Hong Ko

D1019842

Scholastic Canada Ltd.
604 King Street West, Toronto, Ontario M5V 1E1, Canada

Scholastic Inc.
557 Broadway, New York, NY 10012, USA

Scholastic Australia Pty Limited
PO Box 579, Gosford, NSW 2250, Australia

Scholastic New Zealand Limited
Private Bag 94407, Botany, Manukau 2163, New Zealand

Scholastic Children's Books
Euston House, 24 Eversholt Street, London NW1 1DB, UK

Library and Archives Canada Cataloguing in Publication
Hughes, Susan, 1960-
Bailey's visit / by Susan Hughes ; illustrated by Leanne Franson.
(The puppy collection)
ISBN 978-1-4431-2409-6
I. Franson, Leanne II. Title. III. Series: Hughes, Susan,1960- . Puppy collection.
PS8565.U42B35 2013   jC813'.54   C2013-901884-0

Thank you to Dr. Stephanie Avery, DVM, for her puppy expertise.

Cover credits:
Cover: Labrador retriever © AZP Worldwide/Shutterstock.com.
Corners: © Freeroot/Shutterstock.com Logo: © Mat Hayward/Shutterstock.com;
© Michael Pettigrew/Shutterstock.com; © Picture-Pets/Shutterstock.com.
Background: © Ann Precious/Shutterstock.com

6 5 4 3 2 1   Printed in Canada 121   13 14 15 16 17

MIX
Paper from
responsible sources
FSC® C004071
www.fsc.org

For my sister-in-law Carolyne Hughes
and her Bella

Chapter One

Puppies were running across the grass. Dozens of puppies.

Some puppies were black, some were brown, some were white with black spots. One puppy was red and shaggy. Another was grey with a white muzzle. All the puppies had smiling faces and wagging tails.

Kat was sitting on her front steps. Her eyes were closed. She was having her favourite puppy

daydream. And it always ended the same . . .

The puppies jump around, begging for her attention. Her mother and father smile at her.

"Of course you can have a puppy, Katherine," her mom says.

Her dad sweeps out his arm. "Yes, Kat. Pick any one you want!"

Kat smiles, too. She looks at all the puppies, and she tries to choose. The little toffee-coloured Irish terrier that has jumped into her lap? The shy grey schnauzer looking at her, his head cocked to one side? The black pug, so tiny that —

Aidan's running shoe nudged her leg, and Kat opened her eyes. As usual her brother was listening to music. He pulled out one of his ear buds. "Come on, Kat," he said. "Let's go! We're going to be late for school."

Kat sighed. The daydream was over. She sent a mental message to the puppies: *I'll come back and visit soon!*

She ran to catch up with Aidan. The sun was shining. A squirrel chattered at her from the branch of a chestnut tree.

"Do you think Mom and Dad will ever let me get a dog?" Kat asked her brother as they walked.

Aidan shrugged. "You've asked them a million times. They always say no."

"That's because they travel so much for work. But *I* don't!" Kat protested. "And *I'd* be the one looking after the dog."

Aidan bounced his basketball as he walked. "I don't know, Kat. I think you should forget about it for now."

Kat sighed. She knew he would say that. He didn't care if they got a dog. Her parents both liked dogs, but she was the only one who was truly dog crazy.

Kat and Aidan reached school just as the bell rang.

"Later, alligator!" Aidan said to Kat. He hurried over to the grade seven and eight entrance.

"See you soon, baboon!" Kat called after him.

She rushed across the playground. But she didn't get in her lineup. Instead, Kat went over to the other grade four line.

"Maya!" she called. Her best friend hung back as her class made its way into the school.

"There you are, Kat-nip! Late, again!" Maya said, with a grin.

Kat made a funny face at her. Maya had called her "Kat-nip" for as long as she could remember. "You love dogs, but your name is Kat? How goofy!" she'd say. Maya often teased her, and Kat teased her back.

It was all in fun, since they had been best friends forever. Even though they lived at opposite sides of town, they had known each other since nursery school. They played soccer on the same team. They took swimming lessons together.

And, most of all, they talked about dogs together. Maya was probably the only person in the world who loved dogs as much as Kat.

Until this year, Maya and Kat had always been in the same class. But a few children had moved away over the summer. So Maya was put in the grade three-four split class, and Kat was put in the grade four-five split class.

The girls didn't like it. Not one little bit.

School had started last week. The first few days had been tough. Kat hoped it would be better this week, but it didn't seem likely.

"Joke of the day," said Kat. "What does a mother dog call her pups when they come in from playing in the snow?"

Maya thought for a moment. "I don't know. What?"

"I'll tell you at recess!" Kat said, waggling her fingertips at her friend. She turned to run toward her lineup.

"Hey, not fair! Tell me now!" called Maya. "That's torture!"

"Nope! Oh, and I have some really awesome news to tell you," Kat called over her shoulder. "Puppy news!" she added, teasing her friend.

"Seriously? And you won't tell me what it is until recess? You are horrible!" Maya put on her grumpy look, but she couldn't hold it for long. Kat started to laugh, and Maya did, too.

"See you!" Kat called. She ran to the back of her own line, which had just disappeared into the school.

Chapter Two

"So?" Maya asked, running up to Kat at recess. "What does a mother dog call her pups when they come in from playing in the snow?"

Kat grinned. "The answer? Drum roll, please . . . Slush puppies!"

"Agh!" Maya groaned. She had a tennis ball in her hand, and she threw it at Kat. "Take that!"

Kat caught the ball easily and laughed out loud.

She loved telling jokes to Maya. Her friend always responded dramatically, either loving the joke or hating it.

Kat tossed the ball to Maya. They threw it back and forth a few more times.

"Okay, next — the puppy news. What is it?" Maya said.

Kat threw the ball back to her, but her throw was wide. "Oops!"

The ball flew past Maya and onto the field. It landed right in the middle of some boys tossing a football around.

"Uh-oh," Kat said. She went to stand beside Maya.

Then Kat saw Megan and Cora, two girls from her class, pointing at her. They were giggling.

"Nice, Kat," Megan called. "Did you do that on purpose?"

"Do you want to play with your boyfriend?" teased Cora.

"Oh, great," moaned Kat.

"It's your own fault, klutz," said Maya, poking her elbow into Kat's side. "You'd better go get it."

"No way." Kat shook her head. "Not alone."

"Come on. We'll ask your *boyfriend* to give it back to us," said Maya, grabbing Kat's arm and heading toward the field.

"Very funny," said Kat.

She didn't have a boyfriend, and Maya knew it. But one of the boys, Owen, seemed to get all tongue-tied when Kat was around. Sometimes he chased her when the class played tag.

Maya was certain this meant Owen liked Kat.

It seemed like Megan and Cora thought so, too.

But it was Matthew, a boy from Maya's class, who picked up their tennis ball.

As Maya marched Kat toward him, he tossed the ball up and down in his hand.

"Thanks, Matthew," Maya said. "Can you throw it back to us?"

Matthew grinned. He threw it to his buddy Sunjit.

"Sunjit," Kat said. She held out her hands. "Over here. Please?"

"Sure thing," Sunjit said. He tossed the ball to Owen.

Maya and Kat stopped. They both frowned.

"Funny," Maya said.

"So hilarious," Kat added.

Owen blushed.

He froze, looking at them.

Maya nudged Kat. "Basset hound," she whispered.

This was one of the girls' favourite games. They would name a dog breed that a person reminded them of. For example, Kat thought Maya was like an English setter. Elegant. Graceful. Loyal.

Kat looked at Owen.

A basset hound? Yes, she could see it. She began to giggle.

Until Maya softly cooed, "Oh, look at that face. Those lovey-dovey eyes!"

Ugh. No! Kat thought.

"Come on, Owen," yelled Matthew. "Over here. What are you waiting for?"

Owen shrugged and threw the ball to Kat.

"Not back to *them*," Sunjit groaned, smacking his forehead with the palm of his hand.

Maya and Kat laughed and ran back to where they'd been tossing the ball back and forth.

Cora and Megan were still giggling and whispering. Kat tried to ignore them.

"Okay, finally. The puppy news," Maya said. "Spill it. I need to know now!"

And just then, the bell rang.

"Line up, please, students!" called the teacher on yard duty. "No dawdling! To your lines!"

With a moan, Maya grabbed her hair and pulled at it. "I live a life of torment!" she exclaimed.

Kat giggled. Maya would make a great actress!

The girls headed toward the school.

"Okay, okay," Kat said quickly. "Remember I told you my Aunt Jenn was opening a dog-grooming salon?"

"Of course, I remember," Maya replied, rolling her eyes.

The teacher shouted again: "Lines, students! Get in your lines!"

"Well, it's opening today! Aunt Jenn called to let us know last night," said Kat. "My mom and dad are leaving work early, so we can go and see her place after school. And they said you can come with us. If you want."

"That's so cool! We can ask my mom at lunch." Maya looked excited.

The girls took turns going to each other's houses at lunchtime. Today it was Kat's turn to go to Maya's house.

"Miss Reynolds? Do you have somewhere you need to be?" It was the yard duty teacher. She looked at Kat pointedly.

"Right. See you, Maya," Kat said, and off she hurried. She couldn't wait until this afternoon!

Chapter Three

"There it is! Aunt Jenn's place: *Tails Up! Grooming and Boarding*," cried Kat, reading the sign.

She and Maya ran ahead of the rest of the family, past the barber shop, the bank and the hardware store. Then they waited impatiently for everyone to catch up.

Kat's father, Mr. Reynolds, frowned as he came up and read a sign in the store window. "*Walk-ins are welcome.* Don't most dogs walk in?" he asked. "Though, I guess some dogs might have dirty paws, so carrying them in would be better."

"Funny, Dad." Kat grinned. "You know it means that people don't have to make appointments ahead of time. They can just walk in with their dogs."

"Oh, yeah. Right," Mr. Reynolds said, grinning back at her.

But then he frowned for real. "I just hope Jenn can handle it all. Your aunt is a very enthusiastic person — especially when it comes to dogs. I love her dearly. But sometimes she can get a bit carried away with her projects."

"Oh, Robert," said Kat's mother. "You worry too much about your sister! I'm sure she'll be fine. Come on, gang. Let's go in."

"Yeah, let's go," said Kat. She and Maya led the way into Tails Up.

The waiting room had a small couch and three chairs. There was a scale and shelves

lined with bags of dog food. At the front desk was a computer, a cash register and a phone.

There were two customers waiting in the little room. One was a young man who sat with a white Shih Tzu on his lap. The other was a woman with a long-haired Shetland sheepdog, or sheltie, lying at her feet. Both customers looked impatient.

Just then, Aunt Jenn came flying out of a room in the back. She wore a light-blue jacket. Her brown hair was mostly pulled back in a ponytail. A few stray hairs frizzed around her forehead. With her was a thin man holding a tiny chihuahua.

"So, how was she?" the man asked, nervously. "It was Chiquita's first time being groomed."

"She was a natural. Very calm," Aunt Jenn said. "It was a pleasure to groom her."

The man smiled, relieved. He quickly paid his bill and left.

"And, now, hello to you, my loyal family!" Aunt Jenn cried, hurrying toward them with her arms open. She gave each family member a huge hug. "Hello, my Kitty-Kat!" she said. That was her special name for Kat. She lifted Kat right off of her feet!

Then she turned to Maya. "And my most-special niece's most-special friend, you came, too!" And Maya was swept up in a hug, as well.

"The place looks fantastic!" Ms. Reynolds said.

"Yes, well done," Mr. Reynolds added. Aunt Jenn plastered a kiss on his cheek. He patted her on the back awkwardly.

"Oh, it is so nice to have a fan club," Aunt Jenn said, pleased. "Would you all like a tour? This, of course, is the reception area," she said, throwing her arms wide. "When I get a receptionist, this is where she or he will sit."

Mr. Reynolds looked worried. "You haven't hired any help yet?"

Ms. Reynolds poked him. But Aunt Jenn answered cheerfully, "Nope. Can't quite afford it yet."

"Um, excuse me." It was the woman with the sheltie. She was standing now. "I'm Mrs. Fennel, and I have been waiting for quite some time. I believe we are next."

"Oh, Mrs. Fennel," said Aunt Jenn, ruffling Mr. Reynolds's hair. "Don't you think this shaggy guy could use some emergency grooming?" She laughed.

Kat and Maya giggled, too.

Mrs. Fennel frowned. "Oh, well," she said. "No, I meant . . ."

"Your sheltie is beautiful," Kat said quickly. "What's his name?"

Mrs. Fennel's frown vanished. Her face lit up. "Why, thank you. His name is Clarke-Davis."

Clarke-Davis? Kat tried not to giggle again. "I love dogs," she said. "May I pet him?"

"Certainly," the woman replied, pleased.

Kat knelt beside the brown and white dog. Gently she ran her hand over his back. "His hair is so soft," she exclaimed.

"Well, I brush him twice a week. And I have him clipped once a month." The woman turned to Aunt Jenn. "My old groomer moved away last month. I was hoping you might be as good as him, although it's doubtful. No one has ever had a way with Clarke-Davis like Roberto did."

"And what about us?" It was the young man with the Shih Tzu in his lap. His dog was asleep, but he wasn't.

"Mr. Winston, you're welcome to leave Clyde here until I'm ready for him," suggested Aunt Jenn. "I have several kennels in the back room. He'd be quite comfortable there while he waits, and then you won't need to sit here with him."

"Leave Clyde in a kennel?" The man looked horrified. "Never."

"Well, I'll be back in no time," promised Aunt Jenn. "I'm just giving a quick tour."

She pointed to the room that she'd just come out of. "My grooming room."

Kat peeked in. She saw two large grooming tables and two stand dryers. Several grooming brushes, clippers, shavers, shampoo bottles and other equipment were on a table nearby.

Aunt Jenn opened a door to another large room with windows. There were several big kennels in the room. "This is where the dogs waiting to be groomed will stay. If their owners will let them!" She winked at Kat. "And the dogs I board will be lodged here, as well. I guess I could call it the doggy-daycare room."

She pointed to a stairway. "Up there is a big room where I can do some puppy training. And there's a yard out back that I can use, too. So you see? I'm all set!"

"And you're going to live here, too?" Kat's father raised his eyebrows.

"Yup. There's another room upstairs that is now officially my bedroom. And there's a small bathroom and kitchen," said Aunt Jenn.

"Grooming and boarding and training . . . You're planning to do all of these, Jenn?" Mr. Reynolds asked doubtfully.

"Sure am," Aunt Jenn said confidently, with a toss of her ponytail.

Ms. Reynolds gave her husband a look, then turned to his younger sister. "It all looks wonderful," she said firmly.

Aidan pulled out one of his earphones. "Very cool," he agreed, nodding.

"Thanks, Reynolds family!" said Aunt Jenn, with a grin.

As Kat's parents and Aidan went back out to the reception room, Aunt Jenn motioned to Kat and Maya to stay behind. "I don't really want your dad to know this yet, Kat," she said quietly. "He'll just think I'm in over my head. But . . . well, I have a little surprise to show you girls."

Kat and Maya stared at one another. What could it be?

Chapter Four

"Follow me," said Aunt Jenn. She led the girls to the far side of the room. A kennel sat under the window in the sunshine. But it wasn't empty.

"Oh!" Kat breathed.

"A puppy!" said Maya.

A chocolate-brown puppy lay in a corner of the kennel, all curled up, sleeping peacefully. But he must have heard the girls' voices, because just then he woke up.

He lifted his head and looked at the girls with his beautiful green eyes. Then he jumped to his feet and wagged his tail energetically.

Kat's heart melted.

"His name is Bailey," explained Aunt Jenn. "He's a Labrador retriever pup. He's only eight weeks old. His owner, Kelly, has only had him for a few days, but she found out last night that she has to go out of town for three days. There aren't many kennels nearby, and most of them are large. She didn't want to take him to a big kennel. She saw my sign, so she called just this morning to see if I'd take Bailey until she's back." Aunt Jenn shrugged. "Look at him. I just had to say yes!"

Kat looked at the adorable little puppy. She knew exactly what Aunt Jenn meant. That was one of the things she loved about her aunt: she'd do anything to help a dog.

"I'll just have to scoot out here every once in

a while to check on him," said Aunt Jenn. "And then tonight and tomorrow night, I'll bring him up to my bedroom in a crate. It should be fine." It sounded like Aunt Jenn was trying to convince herself.

"Of course, it'll be fine," Kat said.

She slipped her arm around Aunt Jenn's waist as they headed back to the front door. "Tails Up is amazing, Aunt Jenn," said Kat. "And so are you."

"Totally amazing!" said Maya.

"It's like a dream come true, girls," said Aunt Jenn. "Listen, I'm quite busy today — opening day and all — but I'm sure things will settle down by tomorrow. I'll have lots of free time in the days ahead. So, you're welcome to drop by any time and keep me company. We can chat puppies together."

"Tomorrow, after school? Can we come then?" Kat asked, quickly.

"Please?" Maya added.

"Of course," Aunt Jenn said, with a smile.

The girls grinned at each other. It was a plan!

Chapter Five

The next day, Kat and Maya were at Kat's house for lunch.

"So, how are things in your class?" Kat asked. She dipped a carrot stick in peanut butter and chomped on it.

Maya shrugged. "Not bad. The younger kids are a bit of a pain. And I miss you, of course," she added quickly.

Kat nodded. It was okay. Maya was much

more outgoing than she was. Everyone liked Maya, and she made friends quickly. She was probably already good friends with all the girls in her class. But just good friends. Not *best* friends. Kat knew that spot was reserved for her.

Maya swallowed a sip of milk. "What about you?" she asked.

"Megan and Cora are driving me nuts," said Kat. "They won't stop teasing me. About Owen."

Maya made a face. "He totally likes you, Kat," she said.

Kat rolled her eyes. "No, he doesn't!"

"He's always watching you!" Maya replied.

"Whatever. Anyway, I don't mind when you say stuff like that. You're not trying to be mean. But when Megan and Cora say it, it's different. Irritating. They're trying to get to me. They were like this last year, too. But, somehow, with you there, it wasn't as bad."

"Well, maybe you need to think of a way to get back at them," Maya suggested.

"Get back at them?"

"Yeah. You know. Revenge. Payback," Maya said. "Kat, come on. You don't watch enough bad movies. Don't you know? Revenge can be sweet!"

The girls laughed and finished eating. Then Maya said, "Let's go look at puppies!"

"Yes!" Kat cheered. The girls ran to the family's computer in the living room.

They began admiring photo after photo of adorable puppies. There were Afghans and Dobermans, Wheaten terriers and huskies and more! Each one was ridiculously cute.

"If you could have any puppy, what would you pick?" Kat asked Maya. It was the question they always asked each other. What if someday they were allowed to get dogs? They wanted to be ready to choose! But it was so hard. Each time, they gave a different answer.

"Today, I would choose a Bernese mountain dog," Maya replied. She clicked to a photo of a Bernese mountain puppy. His coat was black, white and rust coloured. He looked as soft as a stuffed animal. "I read that they can be very loving. They're also strong and easy to train. You can even teach them to pull a cart!"

Maya pushed the mouse to Kat. "How about

you?" she asked. "What would you choose?"

"This little guy is my favourite," Kat said, clicking to a standard schnauzer puppy. He had perky ears and a curly black coat, and his eyes sparkled with mischief. "Schnauzers are very smart. They even work as police and guard dogs."

"He's so cute! But, really, how could we ever choose just one?" Maya sighed. "There are hundreds of dog breeds. And mixed dogs are adorable, too!"

"And I always change my mind," Kat said. "Do I want a big dog or a small dog? Do I want a really smart dog, or a really loyal one? I'd love a dog that I could pick up and cuddle up with. But I also want one to run with at the park. They are all so different!"

"We'll just have to adopt a bunch of them!" Maya said, laughing.

That's when Kat got an idea.

"Hey, I know!" she said, grabbing Maya's arm. "Let's make a scrapbook. We can call it our Puppy Collection. It will be kind of like having our own puppies right now. We can make a page or two about the puppies we like the most. We can draw pictures — or print out photos — and put them in the scrapbook."

"That's an awesome idea!" Maya said. "And we can write a description about each one. What the puppy looks like, what it likes to do, what kind of care it needs — things like that!" She was just as excited as Kat.

"We can even name our puppies!" Kat looked nervously at her friend. "Or is that too dumb?"

"No, not dumb. Brilliant again, Einstein!" Maya said with a grin.

"I'll ask my mom tonight if we can buy a scrapbook," Kat said. She couldn't wait!

"I think my mom might have some scrapbook supplies we can use." Maya was practically jumping up and down. "Oh, and I have lots of puppy stickers! Let's print out the pictures of today's puppies to get started."

The girls printed out a few pictures and started daydreaming about puppy names.

"What about Schneider for my schnauzer puppy?" Kat asked.

"Schneider the schnauzer — I love it! It's dignified. It will totally suit his moustache!" Maya said. "What about Bernie for my Bernese mountain dog? Too obvious?"

"It has personality!" Kat replied. "I think it suits him. He looks like he'd be fun to play with."

"Hey, are we still planning to go to your aunt's grooming studio after school?" Maya asked.

"Of course," Kat said. "She said we could. Remember?"

Then she sat up straight. She looked at Maya. Her eyes widened.

"Uh-oh," said Maya. She shook her head. "I know that look," she teased Kat. "Trouble."

"No, not trouble," said Kat. "Maya, I have an idea."

"Exactly! See? Trouble!" said Maya, grinning. "Okay, Einstein. What is it?"

"What if we ask Aunt Jenn if we can help out with Bailey? Maybe she'll let us play with him!"

Maya's eyes lit up. "Maybe she'd even let us feed him. Or walk him!"

Kat clapped her hands together. "Oh, Maya, wouldn't that be great?"

"It sure would," said Maya.

"Aunt Jenn knows how much we love puppies. I'm sure she will let us play with Bailey," repeated Kat. "I just know it!"

Chapter Six

When school ended for the day, Kat and Maya hurried to Tails Up.

"Wow, it's even busier than yesterday!" said Maya.

There were no empty chairs in the reception area. A red-haired woman sat with an Irish setter at her feet. An elderly man had two pugs on his lap. A young couple sat together with a basset hound puppy between them. A well-dressed woman sat alone, putting on lipstick and looking into a small compact mirror.

Kat and Maya were just deciding where to stand and wait when the door to the grooming room opened. Out came Aunt Jenn. She was being led by an exuberant cocker spaniel.

"Oh, Portia. You look just wonderful!" cried the woman with newly red lips. The dog licked the woman's hand, her tail sweeping from side to side. "I am impressed, Jenn of Tails Up!" the woman said. She looked at her dog from one side and then the other. "I am very impressed. Portia and I will be back in eight weeks. I'll call to make an appointment. Until then." She handed Aunt Jenn some money and followed her eager spaniel out the door.

"Okey-dokey," said Aunt Jenn. She wiped her brow. She smiled when she noticed Kat and Maya.

Aunt Jenn dropped the money into the cash register. Then she waved the girls toward the doggy-daycare room. She turned toward her customers. "Thank you for your patience," she said in her most professional voice. "I'll just be a moment."

As soon as Aunt Jenn closed the door, she punched the air with her fist. "All right! Can you believe it, girls? It's day two, and there are people and dogs lined up to see me! Actual customers with actual dogs! Just like yesterday!"

"This is so great, Aunt Jenn!" Kat high-fived her aunt.

"It's terrific," said Maya.

Aunt Jenn grinned and did a little shimmy with her hips. Then she admitted, "But you know, Kitty-Kat, your dad was right. I'm swamped. I do need to get an assistant of some kind soon. Very soon! We'll have to wait until then to hang out. Okay, girls?"

She glanced at her watch. "I better get my next pooch in here, pronto."

"Okay, Aunt Jenn," Kat said. "But . . . well, how's Bailey? How's he doing?"

"He's fine," said Aunt Jenn. She smiled at the girls. "But maybe we should check on him."

This time, the chocolate Lab was awake. He yipped when he saw the girls approaching. His whole body wiggled as he wagged his tail.

"I've been in to see him several times today," said Aunt Jenn. "He still sleeps quite a bit because he's so young. But I think he might be a bit lonely."

"Oh, hello, Bailey-boy!" said Kat. She poked her fingers through the bars of the kennel, and the puppy licked them enthusiastically.

Then Kat shot a look at Maya. Her friend gave her a nod and a thumbs-up.

Kat took a deep breath. "Aunt Jenn, can we ask you something? Something important?"

"Of course, Kat," Aunt Jenn replied. "What is it?"

"You know how much Maya and I love puppies, right?" Kat began. "Do you think we could play with Bailey for a little while?"

For a moment, Aunt Jenn didn't say anything. She trained her blue eyes on the girls and studied them carefully. "Puppies are very cute," she said. "I couldn't agree more. But looking after them is a big responsibility. Dogs are very precious. And they are most precious to the people who love them best, their owners. When people bring their dogs here, they are putting a huge amount of trust in me. They need to know that they can count on me to keep their puppies safe and healthy."

Kat nodded, but she felt her heart sink.

Then Aunt Jenn went on. "But I do need help here. That's for certain. I'm a little busier than I thought I'd be!" She yanked out her ponytail and made a new, neater one. She straightened her jacket. "And Bailey could probably use a little more attention than I have been able to give him today."

Kat held her breath. Maya was still, waiting.

"So, I'm going to agree to this," she said.

"Oh, Aunt Jenn! Thank you!" cried Kat. She felt Maya squeeze her hand, and she squeezed it back.

"This is to help Bailey, girls," Aunt Jenn reminded them. "You have to remember that he is not a toy. You need to make sure there's nothing he can chew on that will harm him. You must make sure you handle him gently and don't let him fall."

Aunt Jenn opened the door of Bailey's kennel. As she reached for the puppy, he began wiggling even more. He wanted out!

"You have to be very careful to hold him securely." Aunt Jenn showed them how to lift

Bailey out of the kennel. "Puppies are very wiggly and they can easily wiggle right out of your grasp. As soon as you can, hold him against your own body. That will calm him and give you more control of his little, squirmy body."

Aunt Jenn popped Bailey back in the kennel. "Now, Kat, let me see you do it."

Kat felt a rush of happiness run through her. Carefully she opened the kennel door and reached in. She lifted Bailey just as Aunt Jenn had shown her. She cupped one hand under his rear end and his back legs, and she used the other hand to grip his shoulders and front legs. The puppy wriggled with joy, trying to climb up her arms.

Kat quickly pulled him close, hugging him against her chest. Bailey raised his head and licked her chin. Once, twice.

"Very good," said Aunt Jenn. She looked at her watch again. "Maya, your turn."

Kat put Bailey back in the kennel. She was careful not to get his legs or tail caught on the opening. Then Maya practised. She looked overjoyed to be holding the puppy.

"Well done!" said Aunt Jenn. "I think you've both got it. Now, today you can play with Bailey in this room only. Those are some of his toys." She pointed to a basket. Then she pointed to an area covered with newspaper. "This is where I am house-training Bailey. If you see him peeing or about to pee, please place him on the newspaper. Okay?" She headed to the door.

"Got it," said Maya.

"I'll be back in a bit," said Aunt Jenn. "Remember, don't take him outside. And come and get me if you need anything." Then she rushed back to her customers, and Kat and Maya were alone with the pup.

Chapter Seven

"Hello, little guy," Kat said, softly. She patted the puppy's head. She touched his silky ears. Bailey squirmed and wiggled with delight in Maya's arms.

"Okay, let me put you down, Bailey," Maya said, struggling to hold the excited puppy. She squatted and gently set him on the floor.

Bailey sat on his haunches, smiling up at the girls.

"He's so tiny! Only eight weeks old," said Kat. I've never seen a puppy so young before."

"Me, neither," agreed Maya.

"But look at his paws. They're huge!" Gently Kat lifted one of Bailey's front paws. "That means you're going to be a big dog when you're fully grown," Kat told him.

"Hey, do you think it's true that retrievers have webbed feet?" asked Maya.

"Let's look," said Kat. She and Maya examined the bottom of Bailey's paw closely, spreading it gently.

"Hey, it really is webbed!" said Maya. "That is so cool!"

"I read that most breeds of dog have a bit of webbed skin between their toes, though it's not enough to say they have webbed feet. But some breeds, like retrievers, have more webbing," Kat said. "Retrievers were bred to swim out to fishing nets and bring them back to shore. The webbed feet help them swim."

Restless, Bailey licked Kat's fingers. Then he pulled his paw away. He jumped to his feet and looked at the girls, wagging his tail.

"I think he wants to play!" said Maya.

"Good idea, Bailey," said Kat. "Let's do it!"

For almost an hour, the girls ran and tumbled with the puppy. He chased them, and then they chased him.

Around and around they went. Every once in a while, Bailey flopped down on his tummy and rested.

"Bailey has two speeds: full speed and full stop!" Kat told Maya, laughing.

Other times, the roly-poly puppy would go so fast, he'd lose his balance. He'd do a somersault, head over tail.

Finally, it was the girls' turn to catch their breath. Bailey bowed to them with both front paws out in front. It was as if he were saying, "Come on. Just try and get me!"

"We're taking a break, Bailey!" said Kat.

"Yeah, you're wearing us out!" Maya panted.

Bailey turned and sniffed the other empty kennels. Then he found his big basket of toys. With a giant leap, he scrabbled over the side of the basket. He fell right into the jumble of rubber chew toys and cloth tug ropes. He twisted and turned until he was sitting again.

"Bailey, you're so cute!" Kat laughed.

Bailey grabbed a chew toy between his teeth. He shook it hard from side to side, his ears flying in all directions. Then he lost his balance and toppled over onto the toys again.

Maya giggled. "Oh, Kat, I wish I'd brought my camera! We could add Bailey's photo to our Puppy Collection!"

"Next time, for sure," agreed Kat.

"Kat, do you think there will be a next time? Do you think your Aunt Jenn will let us come and play with Bailey again tomorrow?" asked Maya.

"I sure hope so," said Kat. "If she thinks we've done a good job with Bailey today. We need to prove to her that she can trust us, and that we can keep Bailey safe."

Just then Bailey leapt up. His ears flopped here and there as he looked around his basket. He waded through his toys to the side of the basket, attempting to climb over the edge.

Suddenly the whole basket tipped over. Everything tumbled out — all the toys and the puppy, too!

"Bailey!" Kat cried in alarm. But the little chocolate-brown Lab picked himself up. He gave an enormous shake. The girls both crouched down and clapped their hands.

"Good boy, Bailey!" they cried. "Here, boy!"

At once, Bailey's ears perked up and his eyes brightened. He galloped toward the girls at full puppy speed.

"Whoa, Bailey, slow down!" warned Kat. But

Bailey came barrelling toward them. And when he reached the girls, he couldn't stop! He tried, but his little legs went here and there. Bailey skidded into Kat, who fell back on her bum with a thump, knocking over Maya, as well. Girls and puppy lay in a heap on the floor.

Just then the door to the doggy daycare opened.

"Aunt Jenn," cried Kat, her heart sinking. There was her aunt, frowning, her hands on her hips.

Chapter Eight

"Girls?" Aunt Jenn raised an eyebrow.

Kat and Maya jumped to their feet. Kat reached down and scooped up Bailey. "We're fine. Bailey's fine," Kat said, quickly. "We were just playing. Everything's fine."

"Totally fine," Maya added.

Bailey gave a little happy puppy bark. He squirmed and licked Kat's hands. "See?" Kat said. "Bailey's fine."

Aunt Jenn's face cleared. She grinned. "Okay, that's good. I just thought I'd come and say thanks. It's probably time for Bailey to nap again. I'm sure you've tired him out! He'll be fine now until I close up and can spend the evening with him."

Kat nodded, hugging the sweet puppy close to her.

Aunt Jenn wasn't angry.

She wasn't upset.

She could see that Bailey had been safe with them.

Carefully, Kat and Maya put Bailey back in his kennel.

"Bye, my friend," Kat told him, giving him a last rub on the head.

"Have a good little sleep," said Maya. She kissed the palm of her hand, and then she placed the kiss onto the puppy's head.

"Thanks, girls," said Aunt Jenn. "It looks like you did a great job looking after Bailey today."

Kat and Maya held their breath.

They didn't want to ask. They didn't dare hope. But they couldn't say goodbye until they knew.

"So," continued Aunt Jenn, "do you think you two could come again tomorrow. Maybe Thursday afternoon, as well? Bailey's owner won't be back until that night. I'm sure Bailey would like some playmates, especially if I'm as busy tomorrow as I've been so far."

"We'd love to," said Kat. "Right, Maya?"

"You bet," agreed Maya, with a huge smile.

*

On Wednesday, the girls hurried toward Tails Up right after school.

Kat complained to Maya as they walked.

"Megan and Cora stood behind me in line after recess. Then they started making little kissy noises when we walked back into class," said Kat. "When I turned around, they looked all innocent, and Megan said, 'Oh, Kat, were you looking for Owen?' They are so annoying. Can't they think of anything better to do than bug me?"

Maya shook her head. "I told you. Revenge. An eye for an eye. If they do something mean to you, do something mean back."

Kat shrugged. "Yeah, maybe," she said.

Then all thoughts of school and Megan and Cora vanished — Tails Up was in sight, and there was a lonely little puppy waiting for them!

Once again the reception area was crowded with customers and their dogs. Kat was pleased. Aunt Jenn's business was doing so well!

The girls made a beeline to the doggy-daycare room.

"It's us, your buddies!" Kat called out to Bailey, as they hurried toward his kennel. She saw the puppy jump to his feet and wiggle. He gave excited puppy woofs, asking to come out and play.

"I think Bailey recognizes us!" cried Maya.

Kat lifted up the puppy and gave him the first hug. Then she passed him over to Maya, who covered his head in little kisses.

As soon as Maya set Bailey down, the retriever puppy went off to explore the room again. He sniffed here and there, his tail high. After a while, the girls sat on the floor and rolled Bailey's ball back and forth between them. Bailey raced

after it, excited. The ball was too big for him to hold in his mouth. But he pounced on it like a kitten, and sometimes he managed to trap it between his big puppy paws. The girls laughed while he wrestled with it.

The chocolate-brown puppy had tons of energy, but Kat and Maya were careful to make sure he didn't get into any mischief. He even used his newspaper properly!

Dinnertime came quickly. It was time to put Bailey back in his kennel.

Kat picked him up and snuggled him in her arms, enjoying his puppy smell. The girls stood in the sunshine, looking out the window at the backyard.

The yard was large, and it was surrounded by a chain-link fence. There was a smaller fenced-in area along one side, sort of like a doggy playpen. There were also some bushes and trees for shade.

Kat pointed at a children's wading pool

propped up against the fence. "I bet Aunt Jenn is going to fill that with water for her boarders, one day," she said.

Reluctantly, the girls said goodbye to Bailey. Kat gave the weary puppy a final kiss on the head, and Maya tugged gently on his ears.

"We'll see you again tomorrow, little guy," Maya said.

"Don't worry; we'll be back." Kat put him in his kennel.

"Maybe we should take Bailey outside tomorrow," Maya suggested, as the girls headed home. "I bet he'd love playing on the grass."

"He would," Kat agreed. "And imagine how much fun he'd have splashing around in the pool."

"Well, then, let's do it," Maya said. "Let's take him in the back tomorrow."

Kat shook her head. "Aunt Jenn said we had to stay inside with him, remember?"

"Well, at least let's think about it, okay?" Maya said. "It would be for Bailey, after all. It's his last afternoon with us."

Chapter Nine

All day Thursday, Kat had trouble concentrating on her work. She usually daydreamed about puppies, dozens of them in all sizes and colours. But today there was only one puppy in her thoughts: Bailey.

And the only thing she could picture was how much fun Bailey would have outside. She imagined him rolling in the grass and sniffing at all the outdoor smells. She imagined him free to run full speed from one end of the yard to the other, his ears flying out.

"Kat, are you with us?" asked her teacher.

"Yes, Ms. Mitchell," said Kat, returning to her math problem.

After lunch, it was even worse. The afternoon went so slowly!

When the class was supposed to be working on their stories, Kat found it impossible to keep her mind off Bailey. She couldn't wait to hear his little barks when he saw her and Maya. She couldn't wait to stroke his silky head and tickle his tummy. And the yard? Maybe she would ask Aunt Jenn if she and Maya could take him outside, just for a few minutes.

Kat kept looking at the clock. The more often she looked, the slower the hands seemed to move.

Then Heather, who sat behind her, passed her a note. *Dreaming about Owen?* the note asked.

It had little pink hearts all around it.

Of course, she knew right away who had written it. She looked over at Megan and Cora. The two girls were watching her, their hands over their mouths, giggling.

Angrily, Kat crumpled up the note in her hand.

Then Ms. Mitchell was crouching beside her chair. "Something on your mind today?" she asked Kat, gently.

Kat saw the expressions on Megan's and Cora's faces change. Now they looked scared.

"Yes," she said, nodding. She held the note in the palm of her hand. It would be so easy to show it to Ms. Mitchell. It might finally stop Megan and Cora from teasing her.

"Do you want to tell me about it? Are you missing Maya?" Ms. Mitchell asked.

Kat paused. Maya. It was Maya who had suggested she take revenge on the two girls. Telling Ms. Mitchell about the note would serve them right. They'd probably have to stay in after school. Or they'd have to help out in the kindergarten room at lunchtime. Something.

"Kat?" Ms. Mitchell asked.

Kat wanted to make the girls squirm. But she didn't want to be a tattle-tale. It wasn't like they were bullying her. Not really. And she hadn't even tried telling them to stop.

Kat made up her mind. "My aunt opened her

dog grooming and boarding place in town," she told her teacher. "And I'm helping her by looking after a puppy after school today. His name is Bailey."

"I've seen your aunt's sign. Tails Up, right?" Ms. Mitchell asked.

"That's it!" said Kat, her face lighting up.

"Hmmm . . . That sounds really exciting." Ms. Mitchell knew how much Kat loved puppies. Everyone in the whole school seemed to know! "I have an idea. Since you're supposed to be working on a story now, why don't you write a story about Bailey? That way you can think about him and do your work, all at the same time."

"Okay," said Kat, giving her teacher a smile. "I'll try that."

She picked up her pencil, and right away the words began pouring out. She didn't give Megan and Cora another thought.

Chapter Ten

After school, Kat waited outside for Maya.

When Owen walked past, Kat saw a baseball fall from his pocket.

"Owen, you dropped your ball," Kat said, picking it up for him.

Just then, Megan and Cora walked by. "Kat and Owen, sitting in a tree," Cora chanted.

Megan started to join in.

But Kat had had enough.

"That's it!" she yelled. The girls were surprised. They stopped and looked at her.

"I didn't tell on you in class today. But I still have the note. You need to leave me alone. Owen is *not* my boyfriend," Kat said.

She looked at Owen. His face was completely red. He looked very embarrassed. She hoped she hadn't hurt his feelings.

"But he *is* my friend," Kat added. "And you need to leave him alone, too."

"We were only having fun," Cora said.

"Yeah," said Megan. "You don't have to be so sensitive! Come on, Cora, let's go."

Megan and Cora stomped off across the schoolyard. Kat was shaking. They'd made her so mad!

"I was tired of them bugging me, too," Owen said. "Do you think they'll stop?"

"I think they picked on us because we're quiet. Maybe now that we stood up to them, they'll leave us alone," said Kat. "And, if not, I have proof they've been teasing me. They sent me a note." She smiled and patted her pocket.

"Hi, Kat! Hi Owen!" Maya walked up and beamed at them both.

"Hi, Maya," Owen mumbled, looking at his shoes. "Um, I'd better get going. See you, Kat."

As Owen left, Maya turned to Kat. Her eyes were big.

"What was that about?" she asked.

Kat told her friend about the note Cora and Megan sent her in class. Then she told her how she'd handled it.

"Wow, that's awesome, Kat!" Maya said. "I bet they leave you alone now. You're too fierce to mess with!"

"I hope so. Anyway, we'd better get to Tails Up. Bailey's owner is coming tonight. We don't want to miss our last chance to play with Bailey!"

"Let's go!" said Maya.

***

Kat and Maya watched Bailey as he investigated an empty crate in the doggy daycare.

He tilted his head to one side, then the other. Then he put his front paws up on the side of the crate and tried to climb on top.

The girls giggled as Bailey

toppled over, then bounded up and tried again.

Suddenly Maya said, "Oh, I brought my camera!" She ran to her backpack and got it out. "We can add Bailey to our Puppy Collection!"

"Good thinking!" said Kat. "Hey, maybe we can add the story I wrote about Bailey, too."

"Yeah!" said Maya. "I can't wait to read it."

Maya started snapping shots of Bailey tackling the crate. Then Kat threw a chew toy for the puppy, and Maya took more photos of him playing with it. When Bailey grew tired of the toy, Kat played chase with him, around and around the room. Maya took even more shots.

Then she paused. "It would be so great if we could take Bailey out in the sunshine," she said. "I know we can't," she added, hurriedly. "But wouldn't it be fun?"

"He'd love it," Kat agreed. "Playing on the grass."

"Smelling the bushes and trees," said Maya.

For a moment neither girl said anything.

"I could ask Aunt Jenn," said Kat.

She looked out the window. It was another beautiful day, but it was getting close to dinnertime.

"I'll be right back," she told Maya.

Kat hurried out of the room and into the reception area. A woman with a shaggy sheepdog was speaking to Aunt Jenn. It was almost impossible to tell the front of the dog from the back!

"Not too short, but I don't want the hair left too long, either," the woman said. "Alice prefers it that way."

As the woman bent down to pat her dog, Aunt Jenn looked over her head at Kat and widened her eyes crazily. Kat couldn't help giggling.

"Okay, I think I have the right idea," Aunt Jenn said, gently trying to hurry her along.

But the woman wasn't done yet. Kat had the

feeling she'd been speaking for quite some time.

"Alice is nine years old," the woman said, "and she is quite particular about her hairstyles."

"I see, I see," Aunt Jenn interrupted, politely. "Well, let's take Alice into the grooming room.

I'll get her settled while you continue with your instructions." She slowly guided the woman and her dog toward the grooming room.

As she went, she shot Kat another kooky look and mouthed, "Help me!"

"She's too busy," Kat told Maya, returning to the doggy-daycare room. "I couldn't talk to her."

"Okay," said Maya. She was holding Bailey. "Well, what do you think we should do?"

The girls went over to the window and looked outside.

"Your aunt told us not to take Bailey outside, but that was two days ago. That was on the first day we played with Bailey," Maya reminded Kat. "She probably wasn't sure yet if we were responsible. She was just trying us out."

"Yeah," Kat agreed.

"I bet if you'd asked her now, she would have said yes," Maya said.

"Yeah, maybe," Kat said.

A squirrel searched for food in the back garden, twitching its tail. What would Bailey do if he saw a squirrel? Kat wondered. It made her smile.

"Hey, what did the tree wear to the pool party?" Kat asked Maya.

Maya grinned. "I don't know. What did the tree wear to the pool party?"

"Swimming trunks," said Kat.

Maya groaned loudly. "Not funny," she said.

The girls watched as the squirrel ran up the side of the fence and jumped onto a tree branch. Bailey's ears pricked up.

"You saw that squirrel, too, didn't you, Bailey?" Maya asked with a laugh.

"The backyard looks pretty safe," Kat said. "There's a fence all around it. I doubt Bailey could get into trouble back there." She patted the puppy's head. "What do you think, Bailey? Do you want to go outside?" The puppy began to squirm and whine. Kat and Maya laughed.

"You do want to go outside, don't you, Bailey?" Kat said. "We thought so!"

"What if we take him outside for only a few minutes? Five minutes. We'll time it," said Maya. She showed Kat her watch. "Should we?"

Kat and Maya stared at each other. Should they do it, even though Aunt Jenn had said not to? She'd placed a lot of trust in them. She'd even let them come back and help again because they'd done such a good job the first day. They'd been responsible and taken very good care of Bailey. Then, again, how could going in the backyard possibly hurt the puppy? It would be so much fun for him. Should they?

Chapter Eleven

Suddenly, at exactly the same moment, both girls made up their minds. They blurted out, "No!"

Then they burst out laughing, because they'd surprised each other — speaking at exactly the same time, saying exactly the same thing.

Just then, Aunt Jenn came flying through the door. She was holding her stomach.

"Aunt Jenn! What happened?" cried Kat. She

placed Bailey in Maya's arms and rushed over to her aunt. "Is everything okay? Why aren't you grooming Alice?" she asked, putting her arm around Aunt Jenn's shoulders.

"Girls, some dog people are so funny! Just so funny!" Aunt Jenn's shoulders were shaking. Kat realized her aunt was laughing!

"Alice's owner decided to book an appointment for a different day. She felt Alice was not in the 'right emotional state of mind' to be clipped today," Aunt Jenn laughed harder. "Especially by a groomer she'd never met." She put her hand to her chest. "Oh, my," she gasped. "Oh, my."

Kat and Maya started to laugh along with her.

Suddenly the girls had the same horrible thought. What if they had taken Bailey outside just now? Aunt Jenn would have seen them! What would she have said? What would she have done? Right away, they knew they'd been right to follow Aunt Jenn's directions.

"You came out to speak to me a few minutes ago, Kat. Was there something you wanted?" Aunt Jenn asked.

Kat blushed. "No, not really, Aunt Jenn." Then she added, in a rush, "Other than, we just wanted to say thanks for letting us help out with Bailey, and we hope his owner is pleased that she boarded him here."

Aunt Jenn came over and patted Bailey's head. He looked up at her with his green eyes and smiled.

"Well, girls, there are two things I wanted to tell you. First, there's good news about the backyard. I have someone coming to fix the holes in the fence. You can't see them from here, but there are several large openings behind those trees. A puppy could wiggle under the fence and be gone in a flash! But once the fence is fixed, we can exercise the dogs out there."

Aunt Jenn had said "we"! Kat swallowed hard but didn't say anything. Maya clutched her arm.

"And the second thing: you've really proven yourselves to me. You've done a fine job following instructions, and you've been so good to Bailey. I hope that you'll be able to help me out on a regular basis. Even if I do get an assistant — I know, I know, I need to do that . . ." She waved her hands around.

"Anyway, I wanted to check with you, to make sure you could still come and give me a hand around here."

Kat and Maya beamed.

"We've love to!" Maya cried.

"Thanks so much for asking!" said Kat.

"Well, then, it's a deal. Now, I have to get to the next customer. A super cute little pug that needs his nails clipped," Aunt Jenn said. "I'll see you soon, right?"

"Right, Aunt Jenn," Kat said.

As soon as the door closed behind the groomer, Kat and Maya stared at each other.

"Can you imagine if we'd gone outside with this little guy and he'd escaped?" Kat whispered. "You would have found one of those holes, right, Bailey? You're so clever and such an explorer." She reached out and rubbed his tummy.

"You might have got lost. You might have got hurt . . ." Maya said softly. Bailey lifted his head and licked her chin.

"And Aunt Jenn never would have trusted us again! That would have been terrible," said Kat.

For a moment, the girls didn't speak, and then smiles swept across their faces.

"Kat," Maya said. "We get to come and help out at Tails Up all the time!"

"And we'll have lots more puppies to add to our Puppy Collection!" cried Kat.

"Let's play with Bailey a little bit more before we say goodbye to him," said Maya, setting the squirmy little puppy back down on the ground.

He bounded across the floor toward his knotted rope toy. He grabbed it between his teeth and shook it. Then he threw it up in the air. When it dropped, he ran and pounced on it, and shook it between his teeth again.

The girls laughed in delight.

"I'm going to miss this little guy," Maya said.

"Me, too," said Kat. "But we'll add Bailey to our collection, and then we will always remember him!"

**For more Puppy Collection fun,
check out these other books
in the series.**

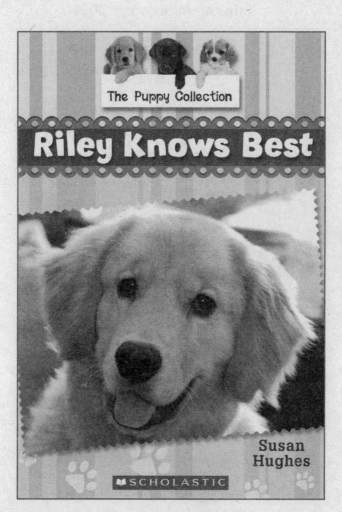

The Puppy Collection

Riley Knows Best

Susan
Hughes

SCHOLASTIC

Coming in Summer 2014!

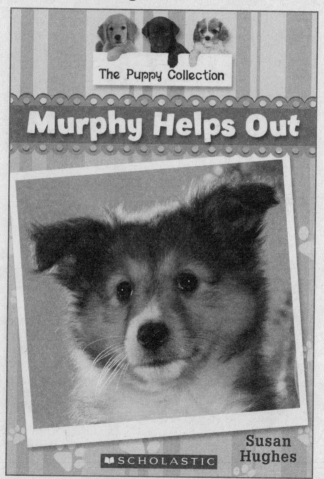

The Puppy Collection

Murphy Helps Out

Susan
Hughes

SCHOLASTIC